Dad for Sale

Andrés Pi Andreu

Illustrated by Enrique Martínez

Play Station 1

 1 Listen and match.

 2 Look and write.

A The .... is in the fish tank.

B The .... is in the dog bed.

C The .... is in the cage.

3 Look, read and match.

A Yes, I've got a mouse.

B Yes, I've got a bird.

C Yes, I've got a cat.

D Yes, I've got a rabbit.

4 Ask and answer with a friend.

Play Station 1

 5 **Look, read and write.**

A I like butter, jam and milk but I don't like ham, eggs and juice.

B I .... ham, eggs and juice but I .... butter, jam and milk.

 6 **Write and draw.**

I like ....
....
but I don't like ....
....

7 Listen and say the chant.
Look, read and tick (✔) or cross (✘).

I like jam, but I don't like butter.
Do you like jam?
Yes, I do!
Do you like butter?
No, I don't.
I like jam but I don't like butter.

I like milk, but I don't like juice.
Do you like milk?
Yes, I do!
Do you like juice?
No, I don't.
I like milk but I don't like juice.

I like ham, but I don't like eggs.
Do you like ham?
Yes, I do!
Do you like eggs?
No, I don't.
I like ham but I don't like eggs.

Jam, milk and ham. Jam milk and ham.
We like jam and milk and ham!

🎧3 "Dad, I don't love you anymore."
"You don't love me?" says Dad.

"No. I want you to leave the house.
I don't want to see you anymore."
"But, why?"

"You don't let me put jam in the fish tank.
At Rosie's house, she can.

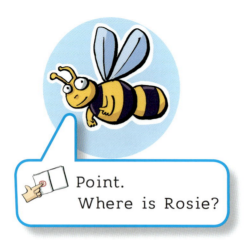

Point.
Where is Rosie?

You don't let me sleep in the dog bed.

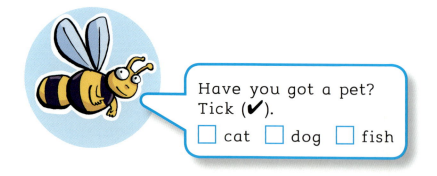

Have you got a pet?
Tick (✔).

☐ cat ☐ dog ☐ fish

But Rosie can.

You don't let me hide my mouse in the fridge. But Rosie can.

What is in your fridge? Tell a friend.

Let's go to the shop, Dad!"
"What shop?"
"The Dad shop. I want to get a new dad."
"What about me?" says Dad.

Where is Dad? Tick (✔).
☐ In the cage.
☐ In the dog bed.
☐ In the fridge.

"Don't worry, Dad. Another child can buy you. I can say that you're good.

What is the boy doing?
Tick (✔).

☐ Climbing a tree.
☐ Playing ball.
☐ Riding a bike.

I can say that you like taking me to the park.

And you like playing with me and buying me toys. And we have lots of fun."

Match.

A He is under ☐ Dad.
B He is on top of ☐ the ball.

"Yes, we have lots of fun."
Dad is sad now. He doesn't want another child.
"But who can buy me at the Dad shop?"

Find:
2 forks   2 plates   3 spoons

"Me, Dad!
Because you're the best
dad in the world!"

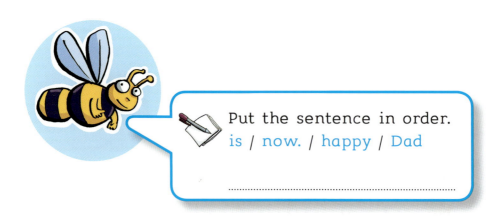

Put the sentence in order.
is / now. / happy / Dad

....

Play Station 2

1 Look, read and put the story in order.

Dad is sad now.

The boy wants to put jam in the fish tank.

The boy wants to put his mouse in the fridge.

The boy says Dad is the best dad in the world.

The boy wants to get a new dad.

The boy wants Dad to leave the house.

2 Look and tell the story to a friend.

 3 **Complete the sentences with the correct verbs.**

go
have
hide
play
put
sleep

A Rosie can .... jam in the fish tank.

B Rosie can .... in the dog bed.

C Rosie can .... her mouse in the fridge.

D The boy can .... to the park with Dad.

E The boy can .... with Dad.

F The boy can .... fun with Dad.

4 **Find 10 words from the book (→↓).**

W	O	R	L	D	H	P
C	H	I	L	D	O	E
T	S	S	A	D	U	F
G	O	O	D	H	S	U
O	F	I	S	H	E	N
F	R	I	D	G	E	P
C	A	G	E	D	O	G

What do the remaining letters spell?
What can you buy there?

___ ____

27

Play Station 2

 5 Listen and match.

○ cleaning
○ cooking
○ doing the shopping
○ playing ball
○ riding a bike
○ sleeping

A
B
C
D
E
F

 6 Look at **5** and mime. Ask a friend.

What am I doing?

You are sleeping.

7 Look, read and write.

cleaning	✗	✗
cooking	✓	✓
doing the shopping	✓	✓
playing ball	✓	✗
riding a bike	✓	✗
sleeping	✗	✓

The boy likes ....

But he doesn't like ....

Dad ....

But he ....

8 Ask a friend.

Do you like cleaning?

Yes, I do.

No, I don't.

Play Station 2

9 Read and match.

A    B    C    D

◯ You can drink this.   ◯ You can clean with this.

◯ You can ride this.   ◯ You can cook with this.

10 Match and put the sentences in order. Then write.

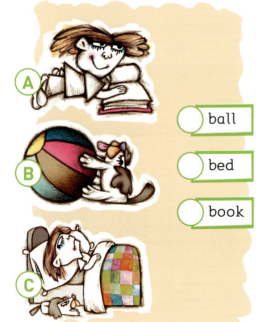

◯ ball
◯ bed
◯ book

1 read / You / this. / can

....

2 this. / You / with / can / play

....

3 sleep / can / in / You / this.

....

11 Look, read and circle.

A	There is a table.	YES	NO
B	There are three chairs.	YES	NO
C	Dad has got a book.	YES	NO
D	The boy has got brown hair.	YES	NO
E	Dad is happy.	YES	NO
F	Dad and the boy are in the bedroom.	YES	NO

 12 Listen and check.

Play Station Project

Badges

Make your own badges.

You need:

paper or card

colours

ruler

scissors

safety pins

glue

sticky tape

1
Use your ruler and divide the card or paper into eight squares.

2
Cut out the eight squares.

3
Ask an adult to put the safety pin through the back of one of the squares.

4
Fix the safety pin on the card with sticky tape.

5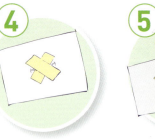
Stick another piece of card on the back to make the front of your badge.

6
Draw and colour a border to decorate your badge.

7
Now write on the badges.

Go to www.helblingyoungreaders.com to download this page.

32